And then it rained...

And then it rained...

by CRESCENT DRAGONWAGON

illustrated by DIANE GREENSEID

ATHENEUM BOOKS FOR YOUNG READERS
NEW YORK LONDON TORONTO SYDNEY SINGAPORE

And then it rained in the city. The rain pounded down from the dark sky, *plum-drum-trum-trum-trumming* onto the canopies of buildings and the roofs of shiny, yellow taxicabs.

The air smelled wet and clean. Little puddle-rivers rushed by the curb, making swirly, curly, twirly moving rainbows of mixed-together water and gasoline.

The whole city was a wet, wild world.
But no one minded.
Everyone was happy it was raining at last.

BRITTA'S BAKERY
FLOWERS
BY
JOYCE

Most people did inside things they had almost forgotten about during the hot, hot sunny weather.

In 3-G, Jerome Katz read a book about dinosaurs. He liked dinosaurs.

In 14-B, Dorothy Arnof picked up a brass box she had bought when she had visited Turkey. She remembered a long bridge over water, and a train conductor with a curled mustache.

In 5-S, Jon Griswold danced as he cleaned his apartment. He turned up his stereo. He bowed to the vacuum cleaner and opened the windows. Cool, fresh air blew through his clean apartment.

In 11-C, Matthew DeWitt read the Bible. "To everything there is a season, and a time for every purpose under heaven," he read.

In 9-F, Lila Pagnoli took out a cookbook, and some milk, salt, flour, and a packet of yeast. She had never made bread before. When the yeast began to bubble in the milk as the cookbook had said it would, she said, "Will you look at that!"

BARNEY'S
BOOKSTORE
BAGELS

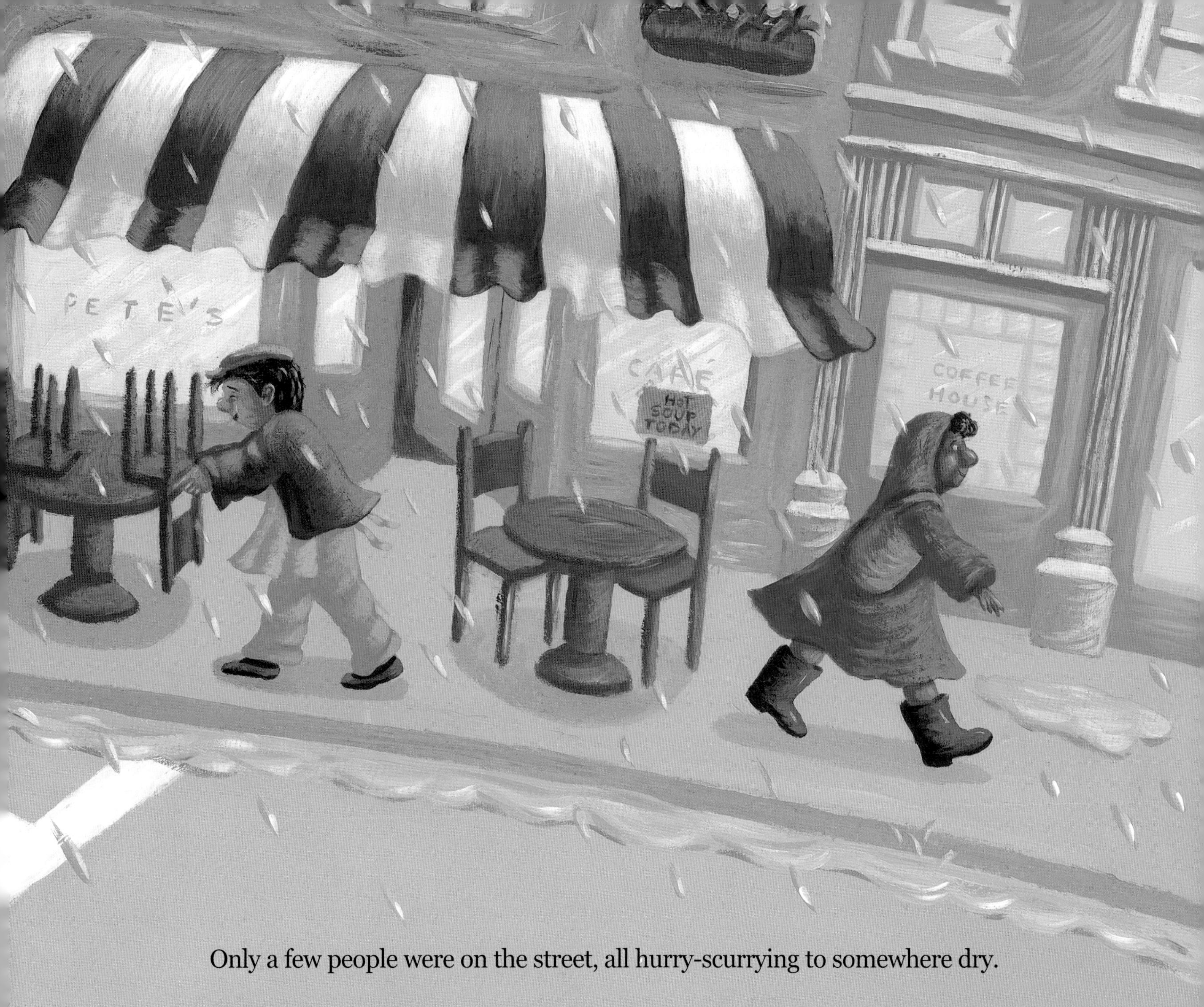

Only a few people were on the street, all hurry-scurrying to somewhere dry.

A waiter moved tables and chairs from the sidewalk of the café to under the awning, turning them upside down. He put a sign in the window that said HOT SOUP TODAY. He knew many people would come to the café to get dry. His tips would be good.

And down the street came someone in a little pair of red rubber boots splish-splashing and kicking in the puddles. A little yellow-covered arm with a small hand reached up high to hold the hand of—

OH! It was a little boy and his father, out walking in the rain.

The two of them stopped to look at the swirly, curly, twirly moving rainbows in the puddles. They listened to the rain pounding from the dark sky, *plum-drum-trum-trum-trumming* onto their rain hats. Their faces were wet, but they were toasty dry in their raincoats. And they smiled at each other.

Then they went into the café and had hot soup.

“I like the rain,” said the little boy happily.

THANK YOU!

Three days passed, then four, then five. And it kept raining. People began to get grouchy.

Jerome Katz got soaking wet when he left 3-G to return the book about dinosaurs to the library. “Do you think it’ll ever stop raining?” he asked the librarian.

When Dorothy Arnof in 14-B woke up and looked out the window, she scowled. “Enough is enough,” she said to herself. The rain made her bones hurt.

In 5-S, Jon Griswold sneezed and coughed. His windows had been closed for days. "This is depressing," he grumbled. "I'm mildewing."

In 11-C, Matthew DeWitt said, "Lord, are You fixing to flood the world again like You did in the time of Noah?"

Lila Pagnoli, in 9-F, thought, *It's a lot easier to get bread at a bakery, but who would go out in such weather?*

The little boy said to his father,
"I'm tired of all this rain. Why won't it stop?"
His father, who liked rhymes, said,

"Rain brings sun and sun brings rain.
Then it turns around again."

The little boy scowled at his father. "I don't *want* a poem," he said crossly. "I want it to stop raining all the time."

His father picked him up and gave him a wet, damp, creaky, squeaky hug.

"Well, my own dear little very wet raincoated boy, I can't say exactly when," said his father. "But I promise you, you will get your weather wish soon."

"I will?" asked the little boy.

"Oh yes," said the father. "I promise."

What happened next? To find out, close the book, flip it over, and see!

*What happened next? To find out,
close the book, flip it over, and see!*

The little boy said to his father, "I'm tired of all this hot sun. Why won't it stop?"

His father, who liked rhymes, said,

> "Rain brings sun and sun brings rain.
> Then it turns around again."

The little boy scowled at his father. "I don't *want* a poem," he said crossly. "I want it to stop being so hot and sunny all the time."

His father picked him up and gave him a hot, sweaty hug.

"Well, my own dear little hot sunny boy, I can't say exactly when," said his father. "But I promise you, you will get your weather wish soon."

"I will?" asked the little boy.

"Oh yes," said his father. "I promise."

In 11-C, Matthew DeWitt said, "Lord, are You fixing to send a plague and locusts along with this drought?" He read his Bible while sitting in front of a fan, which ruffled the pages.

Lila Pagnoli, in 9-F, thought, *Who could eat in such weather?* She ran a cold bath and sat in it until her fingertips wrinkled.

Three days passed, then four, then five. The sun kept shining. It got hotter and hotter and hotter. People got grouchy.

Jerome Katz, in 3-G, took a bus to the library, but the back of his knees stuck to the seat. "Do you think it will ever cool off?" he asked the librarian.

Dorothy Arnof looked out the window of 14-B at the thermometer. It was 101 degrees. "Enough is enough," she said to herself. Too much heat made her tired. *Alaska,* she thought. *No doubt it is pleasantly cool in Anchorage just now.*

In 5-S, Jon Griswold played a song called "It's Too Darn Hot," and closed the curtains. "Too bright, too hot," he complained to himself. "All this sun is fading the upholstery."

The streets were full of people. A man sold falafel from a pushcart. Pigeons pecked at crumbs. The father and the little boy looked at the tiny glints in the sidewalk. They heard the quiet *sus-wus-rus-rus-rustling* of the gentle little wind as it brushed the sunlit leaves of the trees.

The sun was very bright on their faces, but the father and the little boy were wearing sunglasses. Then they went to an outside table at the café and shared a dish of vanilla ice cream. "I like the sun," said the little boy happily.

CAFÉ

OH! It was a little boy and his father, out walking in the sun.

PETE'S

A waiter moved tables and chairs out from under the awning to the sidewalk, turning them right-side up. He smiled. Many people would come out to enjoy the sunny day. The café would be full and busy. His tips would be good.

And down the street came someone in red sneakers, wearing a little pair of overalls. A shirt-covered arm with a small hand reached up high to hold the hand of—

Matthew DeWitt, of 11-C, went out for a walk and whistled “This Little Light of Mine.”

Lila Pagnoli from 9-F passed a businesswoman rushing out of the bakery. The baker shook his head as he wrapped up Lila’s bread. “Everybody’s in a hurry,” he said. “No time to enjoy life.”

“Well, *I* enjoy life,” said Lila. The baker smiled at her, flashing one gold tooth.

“Here, lady, have a macaroon,” he said.

Most people did outside things they had almost forgotten about during the wet, gray, rainy weather.

Jerome Katz put on his sneakers and walked all fifty-seven blocks, from 3-G to the museum, where he visited his favorite dinosaur, Tyrannosaurus rex.

The sun made Dorothy Arnof feel like traveling far from 14-B. *Perhaps Peru,* she thought happily. *I have never been to Peru.*

Jon Griswold locked the door to 5-S and skated three sunny blocks to the gym. In his dance class he smiled at a young woman with a little purple braid.

And then the sun came out. It dried the damp canopies and the rain-washed yellow taxis. A gentle little wind *sus-wus-rus-rus-rustled* down the street, rising and falling and tickling and flapping the scalloped edges of the canopies.

The air smelled dry and fresh. Here and there, sun glinted brightly, lightly bouncing off small sparkly bits of ground-up quartz that were in the pavement. Everything shone.

The whole city was a wide warm golden world.
But no one minded.
Everyone was happy it was sunny at last.

And then the sun
came out...

For George West and Starr Mitchell,

my deeply good friends, in all kinds of weather

—C. D.

To C. B., friend through rain or shine

—D. G.

Atheneum Books for Young Readers
An imprint of Simon & Schuster Children's Publishing Division
1230 Avenue of the Americas
New York, New York 10020

Book design by Abelardo Martínez
The text of this book is set in Georgia.
The illustrations are rendered in acrylic.
Manufactured in China
First Edition
2 4 6 8 10 9 7 5 3 1
Library of Congress Cataloging-in-Publication Data
Dragonwagon, Crescent.
And then it rained . . . / Crescent Dragonwagon ; illustrated by Diane Greenseid.
p. cm.
Summary: Describes how different people react to days of rain and days of hot sun.
ISBN 0-689-81884-X
[1. Rain and rainfall—Fiction. 2. Sunshine—Fiction. 3. City and town life—Fiction.]
I. Greenseid, Diane, ill. II. Title.
PZ7. D7824 Th 2003
[E]—dc21 2002002169

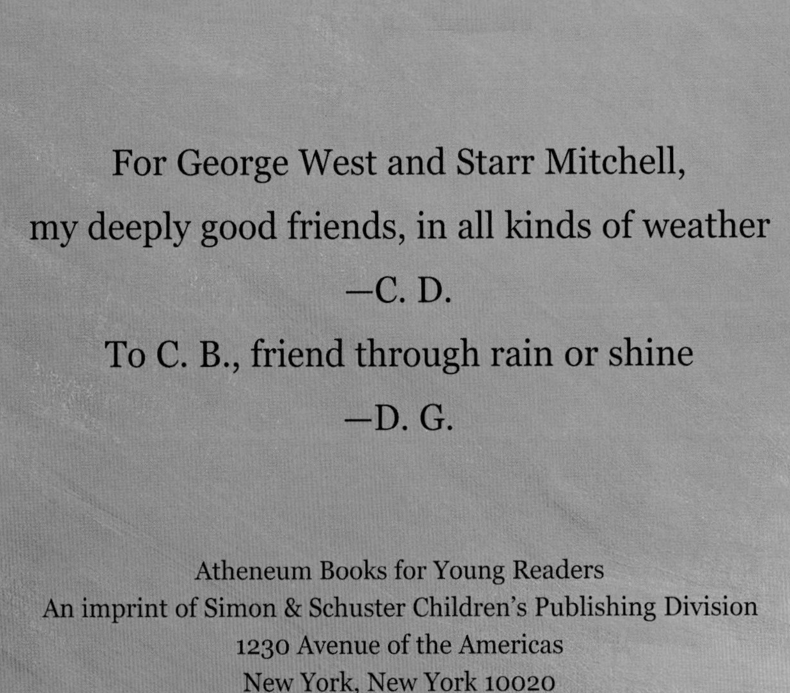